Courtney Crumrin

By Ted Naifeh

The Witch Next Door

Written & Illustrated by

TED NAIFEH

Colored by

WARREN WUCINICH

Original Series edited by

JILL BEATON

Collection edited by

ROBIN HERRERA

Design by

KEITH WOOD AND KATE Z. STONE

Oni Press, Inc.
founder & chief financial officer, JOE NOZEMACK
publisher, JAMES LUCAS JONES
editor in chief, SARAH GAYDOS
v.p. of creative & business development, CHARLIE CHU
director of operations, BRAD ROOKS
director of publicity, MELISSA MESZAROS
director of sales, MARGOT WOOD
marketing design manager, SANDY TANAKA
special projects manager, AMBER O'NEILL
director of design & production, TROY LOOK
senior graphic designer, KATE Z. STONE
graphic designer, SONJA SYNAK
digital prepress lead, ANGIE KNOWLES
senior editor, ROBIN HERRERA
senior editor, ARI YARWOOD
associate editor, DESIREE WILSON
editorial assistant, KATE LIGHT
executive assistant, MICHELLE NGUYEN
logistics associate, JUNG LEE

Originally published as issues 1-5 of the Oni Press comic series *Courtney Crumrin.*

1319 SE Martin Luther King Jr. Blvd.
Suite 240
Portland, OR 97214

onipress.com · tednaifeh.com
facebook.com/onipress · twitter.com/onipress
onipress.tumblr.com · instagram.com/onipress

First Edition: June 2019

ISBN 978-1-62010-640-2
eISBN 978-1-62010-039-4

1 3 5 7 9 10 8 6 4 2

Library of Congress Control Number: 2013916421

Printed in China.

For Jill and James

Chapter One

THERE'S SOMEONE HERE WHO'D LIKE TO THANK YOU PROPERLY FOR YOUR BRAVERY LAST NIGHT.
WHAT ARE YOU TALKING ABOUT-
COURTNEY, THIS IS SKARROW.
HE'LL BE STAYING AS MY GUEST FOR A WHILE. WHY DON'T YOU TWO GET ACQUAINTED?
SO, ERR...
WHAT'S IT LIKE BEING A FAERIE?
DON'T TALK MUCH, DO YOU?

I'VE BEEN DOWN THERE. NOT A GOOD PLACE FOR US MORTALS.
BUT IT WAS PRETTY NEAT. IF THAT'S WHERE YOU BELONG, I DON'T SEE WHY YOU'D LEAVE TO COME UP HERE.
I GUESS IT GETS LONELY DOWN THERE TOO.
ISN'T THERE ANYWHERE THAT ISN'T LONELY?

BUT THAT WAS A LONG TIME AGO, AND SKARROW WAS GONE NOW.

AND COURTNEY STILL LONGED FOR AN ANSWER.

THE AUCTION IS *SUNDAY*, IF YOU'RE *INTERESTED*.

SHE HAD NO *WILL*. THE PROCEEDS GO TO THE *HALL*.
YOU THINK SHE'S *DEAD*?
I THINK SHE'S GOT *NOTHING* TO COME *BACK* FOR.

YOU NEVER *FORGAVE* ME, *DID YOU*?
IT WAS MORE THAN *HALF A CENTURY* AGO, ALOYSIUS. BELIEVE IT OR *NOT*, I'VE LET IT *PASS*.

GOODNESS, BUT THAT MAKES ME FEEL OLD.
I WISH YOU'D TELL ME THE CRUMRIN SECRET. YOU OBVIOUSLY TOLD HER.
HEH, YOU'LL BURY US ALL, I SUPPOSE.
I'M DYING.
DIARY
Sat. 6th June– Woodrue compliments my beauty again and again, as though it were the achievement of many years diligent application.

He's so uncomfortable with it. Sometimes I wish I could put it away in a drawer when it upsets people.
We parted with relief. Our families call us a good match. I wonder if we'll start feeling something soon. Other than nerves.
I suppose I'm old enough now to leave the house after dark by the front door, but old habits die hard.
When I was young, I pretended I was a changeling, abandoned by the Twilight Queen for being too ugly.

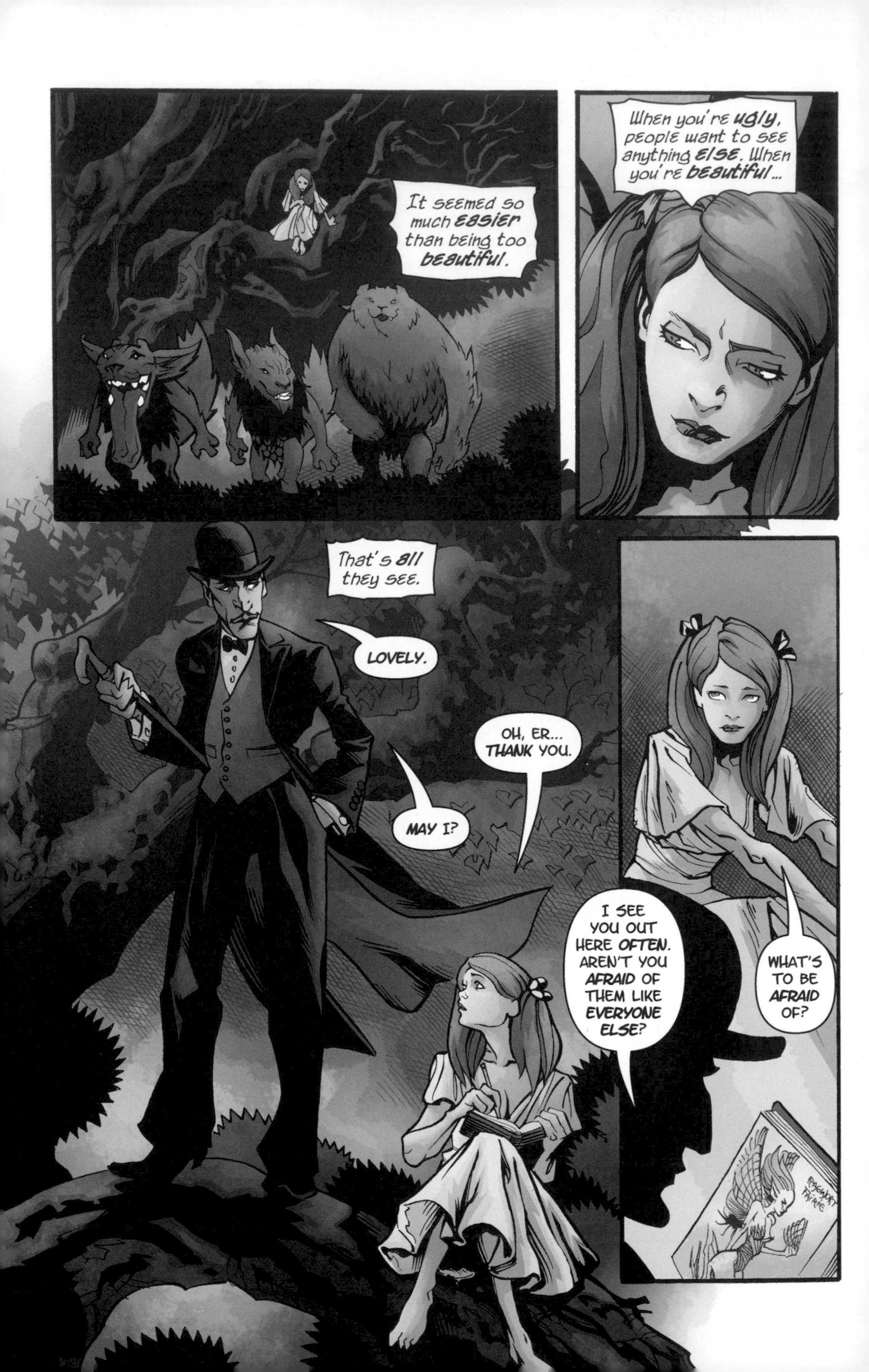
It seemed so much easier than being too beautiful.
When you're ugly, people want to see anything else. When you're beautiful...
That's all they see.
LOVELY.
OH, ER... THANK YOU.
MAY I?
I SEE YOU OUT HERE OFTEN. AREN'T YOU AFRAID OF THEM LIKE EVERYONE ELSE?
WHAT'S TO BE AFRAID OF?

THAT'S WHAT I KEEP SAYING.
BUTTER-WORM
We talked about the night things I'd befriended, and the ones I'd avoided, and the ones I dreamed of encountering.
He wasn't courting me. He wasn't even being polite. He was genuinely interested.
I can't remember the last time I'd felt listened to rather than looked at.
Of course, I knew who he was. The last Crumrin in Hillsborough, who stayed in that crumbling old house even after all the others drifted away.

Sun. 7th June-
One thing I learned early in life is that nothing in this house belongs to me.
That includes the clothes on my back, the contents of my diary...
Even the thoughts in my head.
I HOPE YOU DIDN'T THINK YOU COULD KEEP LAST NIGHT'S LITTLE TRYST TO YOURSELF.
OF COURSE NOT, FATHER.
MY OFFICE, PLEASE.
At first I thought I was in for a thrashing. I'd be humiliated in front of Woodrue, and the world would return to normal.
Instead, things took a turn for the downright sinister.
GENTLEMEN, THANK YOU FOR COMING.
I HAVE SOME INTERESTING NEWS.
IT SEEMS WE HAVE INADVERTENTLY FOUND A WAY TO PROGRESS.

I DON'T UNDERSTAND.
WOODRUE, SINCE YOU BROUGHT THIS TO MY ATTENTION, AND SINCE YOU'LL SOON BECOME MY SON, I FEEL I SHOULD BRING YOU UP TO SPEED.
WHILE WE IDLE AWAY OUR LIVES IN THIS COMFORTABLE BOROUGH, WAR RAVAGES THE WORLD.
THIS IS NOTHING NEW.
WE SORCERERS HAVE SAT BY AND WATCHED THIS COUNTRY ENDURE DEPRESSIONS, WARS, POVERTY, AND MORAL DEGRADATION...
...AS THOUGH WE WERE NOT UNIQUELY CAPABLE OF STOPPING IT.
BUT THE LAW FORBIDS US TO INTERFERE...
INDEED SO. THE COVEN'S LAWS ARE STRICT AND PRECISE.
WE MAY NOT TAKE MAGIC OUT OF HILLSBOROUGH, NOR USE IT TO DOMINATE ORDINARY FOLK.
EVER WONDER WHO MADE THE LAW?

WHEN THE SETTLERS CAME TO THIS LAND, THEY FOUND RAVANNA, DRESSED IN RAGS, LIVING IN A CAVE IN THE WOODS. THEY TOOK HER IN, AND SHE TAUGHT THEM THE CRAFT.
SHE WAS A WILD, HALF-FAERIE CREATURE. WHO KNOWS WHERE SHE CAME FROM?
IT REQUIRED THE IRON WILL OF COLONEL FORREST CRUMRIN, A FORMER CONFEDERATE SOLDIER, TO TAME HER.
SHE TOOK A RESPECTABLE NAME, AND EVENTUALLY BECAME HIS WIFE.
AFTER COLONEL CRUMRIN DIED, IT CAME TO HER EARS SOME OF THE TOWN FOLK WERE TALKING ABOUT USING MAGIC TO SEEK FORTUNE IN THE WIDER WORLD.

IT WASN'T LILLIAN CRUMRIN, RESPECTABLE WIDOW, WHO STORMED INTO THAT TOWN HALL MEETING, BUT RAVANNA, THE WILD HALF-FAERIE WITCH.
SHE LAID DOWN THE LAW RIGHT THEN AND THERE. NO ONE DARED ARGUE.
THEN TO EVERYONE'S GREAT SURPRISE, SHE DIED. WE THOUGHT THE OLD GOAT WOULD LIVE FOREVER.
OH, THEY DISCUSSED CHANGING THE LAW. A FEW LEFT TOWN QUIETLY.
ALL THAT CAME BACK WAS THE RUMOR OF THEIR BITTER ENDS.
IT SEEMS A CURSE WAS LAID ON THOSE WHO VIOLATED RAVANNA'S LAW.

BUT I DIDN'T BELIEVE IT. I'VE MADE A STUDY OF CURSES AND HEXES. THEY'RE GREATLY MISUNDERSTOOD.
AND RELY TOO HEAVILY ON THE FEAR OF THE VICTIM.
I HAVE ANOTHER THEORY.
ALL VERY INTERESTING SIR, BUT WHAT DOES THIS HAVE TO DO WITH ALOYSIUS CRUMRIN? OR HERMIA?
DON'T YOU SEE?
CRUMRIN IS THE CURSE.
I'VE WATCHED HIM OVER THE YEARS, SLIPPING AWAY IN SECRET, SOMETIMES FOR MONTHS.
I FIRMLY BELIEVE HIM TO BE AN ASSASSIN OF SORCERERS.
WHICH BRINGS ME TO HERMIA.
YOU, MY DEAR, HAVE MANAGED TO CATCH THE EYE OF THE MOST SECRETIVE WARLOCK IN HILLSBOROUGH.
EVEN YOU MUST SEE THE OPPORTUNITY.

I felt sick. I turned to Woodrue, but he was no help. He'd do anything for Father's approval.
So there I sat, waiting for Aloysius to appear. I would throw myself at him like a fool, be rejected, and that would be that.
Suddenly, all thought of Aloysius vanished.
I'd never heard of any night thing LIKE it. So beautiful and deadly...
I wondered what it was hunting, and hoped it wasn't me...

Then I realized-
I felt pulled into the wake of the creature. I had no idea what I hoped to accomplish.
I'd only seen his eyes for a second.
But I knew I must help him.

My stomach lurched when I saw Aloysius.
His EYES told me he faced death itself.
Then suddenly...
Death blinked.
AH, MISS HARKEN. I'M GLAD YOU'RE HERE.

HE'S HAD A TRYING EVENING.
I doctored his wounds while Aloysius played nurse, following my instructions wordlessly.
HE'LL BE FINE IN A FEW DAYS.
SHALL I MAKE SOME COCOA?
I'd never felt so at ease. How could such a gentle man be an assassin?
DELICIOUS. IS IT MAGICAL?
MMMM. THE CAYENNE PEPPER IS WHAT DOES IT.

Tuesday, 9th June- I considered keeping that night a secret, but Woodrue, Father's faithful servant, had spied the whole thing.
Father was overjoyed.
I COULDN'T HAVE PLANNED IT BETTER. NOW...
TONIGHT, YOU WILL PLACE THIS UNDER HIS PILLOW.
WHAT IS IT?
A POWERFUL LOVE CHARM. I ENCHANTED IT MYSELF.
What can I do, trapped as I am between my father and my fiancé?
Wednesday, 10th June- I returned, pretending only to look in on my patient.

HERMIA?
I BEG YOUR PARDON. I THOUGHT YOU WERE UPSTAIRS.
I'M SORRY, ALOYSIUS. I CAN'T IMAGINE WHAT YOU MUST THINK OF ME.
ON THE CONTRARY. I ADMIRE ANYONE BRAVE ENOUGH TO FOLLOW THEIR HEART.
What fools men are, seeing only what they want to see.
I suppose they're just like us.
SO, IT'S TRUE.
NOT ONLY WAS HE RESPONSIBLE FOR THESE DEATHS, HE INVOLVED ORDINARY FOLK IN HIS MISDEEDS.

FROM WHAT I READ, THOSE SORCERERS HAD SIGNIFICANT MISDEEDS TO THEIR CREDIT AS WELL.
MY DEAR, YOUR TASK WAS TO FETCH THIS EVIDENCE, NOT TO READ IT.

DOES OUR ENGAGEMENT MEAN NOTHING TO YOU?

IF YOU'LL RECALL, IT WAS YOU WHO DREW ME INTO THIS BUSINESS.
YOU COULD HAVE SAID NO. I NEVER THOUGHT IT'D GO THIS FAR.

YOU MIGHT WOUND HIM IN WAYS NO MAN CAN HEAL FROM.
LET'S HOPE SO.
THIS IS NO TIME TO LOSE YOUR NERVE, BOY. TONIGHT, HERMIA WILL FIND A WAY TO ALLOW ME ENTRANCE INTO CRUMRIN HOUSE.
THE WORLD AWAITS US, WOODRUE. AND IF ALOYSIUS CRUMRIN STANDS IN MY WAY...
I WILL DESTROY HIM.

I sent Aloysius into the woods to gather medicinal herbs for Skarrow. He went dutifully, trusting in my expertise.
My father waited at the back door. I led him to the heart of the house.
HIS INNER SANCTUM. WHAT SECRETS MUST IT HOLD, I WONDER?
HIERONYMUS HARKEN, YOU'RE UNDER ARREST.
HERMIA! HOW COULD YOU BE SO FOOLISH?
DON'T BLAME HER, HARKEN.
YOU BETRAYED ME? YOU!?!
WHY SO SURPRISED?
YOU WATCHED ME BETRAY YOUR DAUGHTER, DIDN'T YOU?

YOU MUST HATE ME.
NO.
I JUST WANT TO KNOW...
IF YOU REALLY FELT ANYTHING.
I FELT ASHAMED.
THAT IS HOW I DEAL WITH BETRAYAL, GENTLEMEN!

LET HIM COME FOR ME IF HE DARES. I'LL BE READY.

Everything in me wanted to beg forgiveness, to be taken back.
But what a fool I would look, after all I'd done?
Loneliness was what I deserved.
OH. HELLO.
LOOKS LIKE IT'S JUST YOU AND ME, MISTER.
WOULD YOU HAVE TAKEN HER BACK?

WOULD YOU?
IN A SECOND, OLD BOY. IN A SECOND.
SHE NEVER ASKED, DID SHE?
SUCH A SHAME. DID YOU KNOW MADAME HARKEN?
NOT REALLY. BUT I SUPPOSE SHE HAD A GOOD HEART, DEEP DOWN.
HMPH! FAT LOT OF GOOD THAT DOES IF YOU HAVEN'T THE COURAGE TO USE IT.
YOU WASTE AWAY YOUR LIFE UNTIL, WHEN YOU REALIZE WHAT YOU MISSED, IT'S FAR TOO LATE.
HAVE YOU SEEN THIS LADY? SHE LOOKS TO ME LIKE SHE HAS PLENTY OF TIME.
NOT ANYMORE.

Chapter Two

I'VE ALWAYS HEARD THAT IF YOU DON'T HAVE ANYTHING NICE TO SAY, YOU SHOULD KEEP YOUR MOUTH SHUT. SO I WON'T SAY ANYTHING ABOUT THE POLITICAL THRILLER THAT MADE HOLLY HART'S FATHER A RICH MAN.
ESCROW CLOSES TODAY. IT'S OURS. ISN'T IT PERFECT?
OH, RYAN! YOU CAN ALMOST SMELL THE OLD MONEY AROUND HERE.
I THINK THAT'S THE HOUSE NEXT DOOR.
HIS AGENT HAD WARNED HIM AGAINST GETTING TOO USED TO SUCCESS, IN CASE THE LITERARY WORLD CAME TO ITS SENSES. BUT RYAN HART WAS NEVER ONE TO TAKE ADVICE.
AND IT MAY BE DRY ROT. I UNDERSTAND THEY SMELL SIMILAR.
OH YEAH. UNFORTUNATELY, THAT'S HOW I WAS ABLE TO AFFORD THIS PLACE. BELONGS TO SOME ECCENTRIC OLD PROFESSOR AND HIS FAMILY.
CRUMRIN, I THINK THE NAME WAS.
WHICH IS HOW HOLLY FOUND HERSELF LIVING NEXT DOOR TO COURTNEY CRUMRIN.
WHAT AN EYESORE. MAYBE WE CAN COMPLAIN TO SOME NEIGHBOR-HOOD COMMITTEE.
ACTUALLY, I KINDA LIKE IT.

ORDINARILY, THE "TWEEN" POPULATION OF HILLSBOROUGH WERE READY ENOUGH TO ACCEPT A NEW ADDITION TO THEIR CADRE, ESPECIALLY IF HER FATHER'S LATEST BOOK WAS BEING DEVELOPED FOR A FEATURE FILM WITH LOTS OF EXPENSIVE EXPLOSIONS.
LOOK AT THOSE CLOTHES.
LOOKS LIKE SHE MADE THEM HERSELF. WHAT IS SHE, A REFUGEE OR SOMETHING?
FROM GLOOM-LAND, MAYBE. YOU'D THINK SHE'S NEVER HEARD OF, LIKE, COLOR.
BUT HOLLY KNEW SHE WAS THE SORT OF PERSON WHO INEVITABLY FELL INTO THE CATEGORY MARKED "OUTSIDER."
SO SHE HARDLY FOUND HER RECEPTION SURPRISING.
FINE, SHOW ME THE WAY TO THE LOSER TABLE. I KNOW MY PLACE.
BINGO.
I WOULDN'T SIT THERE.

THAT'S COURTNEY CRUMRIN. WE ALL STAY AWAY FROM HER.
WHY?
SHE'S...
BAD NEWS!
WHAT, LIKE A BULLY? SHE'S PRETTY RUNTY. I'M PRETTY SURE I COULD TAKE HER.
NO. SHE'S...
SHE'S LIKE...
A WITCH.
OR SOMETHING.
OKAAAAY-THANKS-BYE.
SORRY, LOOKS LIKE I'M RUINING YOUR GRIM LONER ROUTINE.
WHATEVER.
SO WHAT'S THE DEAL? WHY DOESN'T ANYONE SIT WITH YOU?
CAUSE THAT'S THE WAY I LIKE IT.

HEY LOOK, I'LL LEAVE YOU ALONE IF-
NO, IT'S COOL.
BELIEVE ME, YOU'LL UNDERSTAND ONCE YOU GET TO KNOW THESE BRAINFARTS.
HAH, YEAH. SOME CHICK JUST TOLD ME YOU'RE A WITCH.
WHAT'S THAT ALL ABOUT?
POP
OOOKAYYY... I THINK I SEE A PATCH OF FLOOR NEXT TO SOME MOLDY BREAD THAT MIGHT BE BETTER COMPANY.
SEE YA 'ROUND.

HOLLY HAD TRIED TO BE OPTIMISTIC ABOUT HER NEW SCHOOL.
BUT NOW ANOTHER LONG, LONELY YEAR SEEMED TO STRETCH OUT BEFORE HER.
SAME OLD ISOLATION, AND IT LOOKED LIKE THE SAME OLD BULLIES.
HOW BORING.
SHE FOUND HERSELF WISHING FOR SOMETHING, ANYTHING, NEW.
MISSING
WE DON'T GO IN THE WOODS. NO ONE DOES.
WHY, WHAT'S IN THERE?
I DON'T KNOW.
BUT THAT KID WENT IN ONCE AND NEVER CAME OUT.
MISSING
THAT'S YOUR STORY?
A COMATOSE CHIMP COULD DO BETTER.

IT WAS A GAME SHE KNEW WELL, CALLED "LET'S MESS WITH THE NEW KID."
SHE COULD HEAR SOMEONE FOLLOWING HER EVEN NOW. THEY WOULD TRY TO GET HER GOOD AND SCARED, AND PROBABLY KNOCK HER AROUND FOR GOOD MEASURE.
SHE KNEW THE ROUTINE BY HEART. KIDS LIKE THAT PICK ON YOU TILL THEY GET CAUGHT...
...OR TILL YOU TEACH THEM A HARD LESSON.
ALRIGHT, FARM GIRL, LET'S DO THIS.
TRICK OR-
-TREAT...?
CRUNCH

NOT BAD, BUT BIT *TOUGH* FER MY TASTES.
I PREFERS MORE *TENDER*-
MERG!?!
BUTTERWORM!
I THOUGHT I *TOLD* YOU, *HUMANS* ARE *OFF LIMITS*.
BUGGER *OFF*.
I WEREN'T GONNA EAT *ALL* O' HER. JUST A FEW *BITS*.

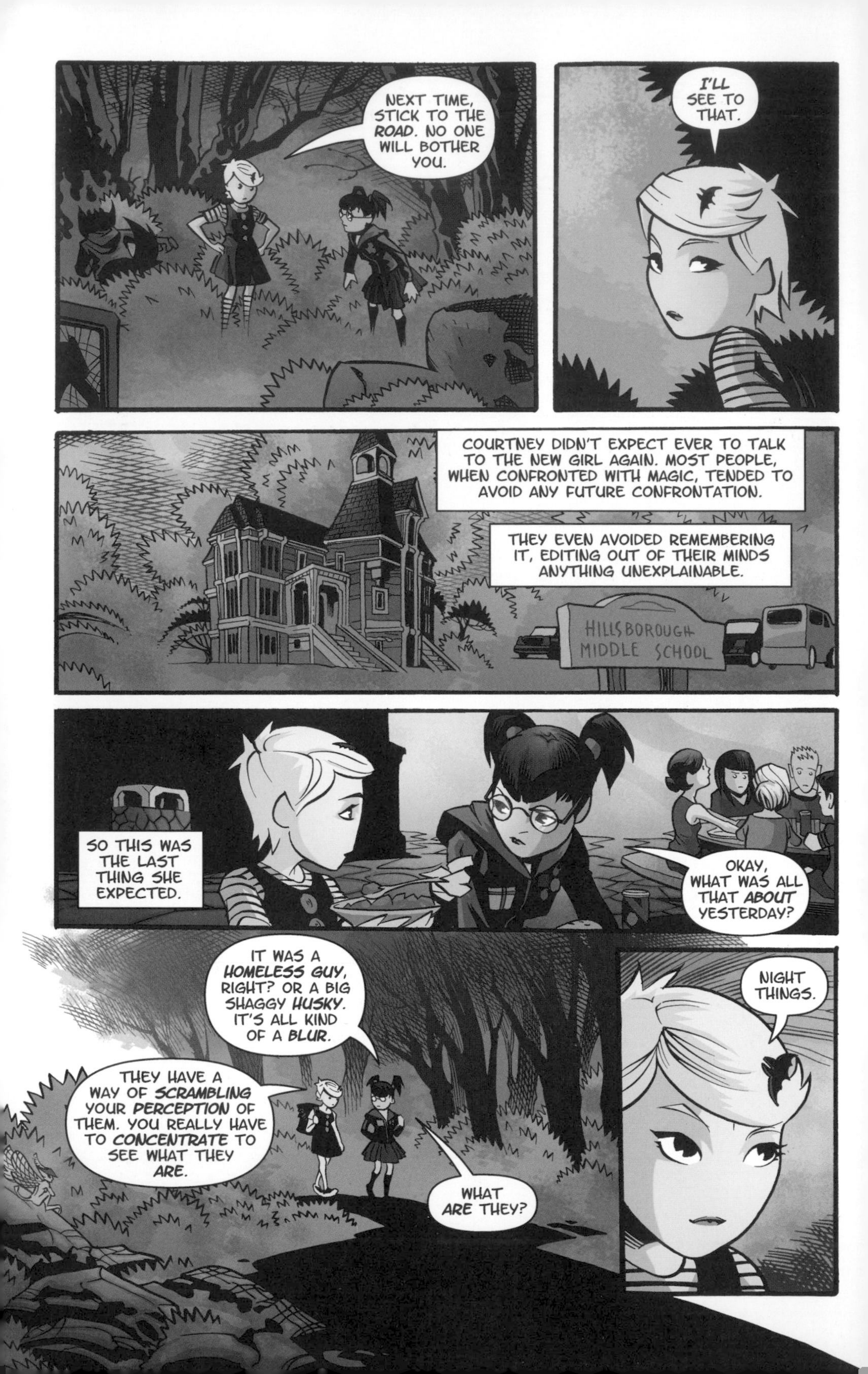
NEXT TIME, STICK TO THE ROAD. NO ONE WILL BOTHER YOU.
I'LL SEE TO THAT.
COURTNEY DIDN'T EXPECT EVER TO TALK TO THE NEW GIRL AGAIN. MOST PEOPLE, WHEN CONFRONTED WITH MAGIC, TENDED TO AVOID ANY FUTURE CONFRONTATION.
THEY EVEN AVOIDED REMEMBERING IT, EDITING OUT OF THEIR MINDS ANYTHING UNEXPLAINABLE.
HILLSBOROUGH MIDDLE SCHOOL
SO THIS WAS THE LAST THING SHE EXPECTED.
OKAY, WHAT WAS ALL THAT ABOUT YESTERDAY?
IT WAS A HOMELESS GUY, RIGHT? OR A BIG SHAGGY HUSKY. IT'S ALL KIND OF A BLUR.
THEY HAVE A WAY OF SCRAMBLING YOUR PERCEPTION OF THEM. YOU REALLY HAVE TO CONCENTRATE TO SEE WHAT THEY ARE.
WHAT ARE THEY?
NIGHT THINGS.

WHAT, LIKE MONSTERS? LIKE THE THING UNDER THE BED?
SORTA.
HERE, THIS'LL HELP.
A MAGIC STONE? YOU PUNKING ME?
JUST TAKE A LOOK.
WOW!
IT'S NOT MAGIC. JUST THE OPPOSITE.
IT LETS YOU SEE WHAT'S REALLY THERE.

AND HERE WAS ANOTHER KIND OF MAGIC. COURTNEY GOT ALONG OKAY WITH THE OTHER KIDS IN THE COVEN, AND SHE FELT AS CLOSE TO HER UNCLE ALOYSIUS AS ONE CAN WITH ANYONE A HUNDRED YEARS OLDER.
YOU'VE LEARNED A LOT OF THESE SPELLS?
A FEW.
AND YOU INHERITED MAGIC FROM YOUR GREAT UNCLE?
NOT EXACTLY. HE SAYS IT'S LIKE MUSIC. ANYONE CAN LEARN TO PLAY A TUNE, BUT SOME PEOPLE HAVE MORE TALENT THAN OTHERS.
BUT IT HAD BEEN YEARS SINCE SHE FELT SO AT EASE WITH ANYONE.
SO I COULD LEARN MAGIC?
I DON'T SEE WHY NOT.
THEY JUST CLICKED.
WHAT ABOUT THIS ONE?
OH. ERRR...
OF COURSE, THAT'S WHEN IT ALL STARTED TO GO WRONG.
YEAH, IT'S NOT HARD. BUT THE THING IS...

...BEING THE MOST POPULAR KID IN SCHOOL SOUNDS LIKE A GOOD DEAL...
HARTLEY
...BUT IT CAN GO HORRIBLY WRONG. TRUST ME.
"WELL, I SPOKE TO THE COUNCIL, AND GAVE THEM YOUR RESEARCH. THEY AGREED TO CONSIDER THE MATTER.
"BUT THEY'RE FAR FROM CONFIDENT THEY CAN RECREATE LADY ISOLDE'S ELIXIR VITAE."
HARDLY SURPISING. THAT CREW WOULD HAVE TROUBLE FINDING THEIR OWN BOTTOMS WITHOUT A MAP.
SO THERE'S NO HOPE? THE GREATEST WARLOCK ALIVE CANNOT FEND OFF THE REAPER?

SURELY THERE'S SOMETHING, HOWEVER DRASTIC.
NECROMANCY, YOU MEAN?
DON'T BE SO OLD-FASHIONED.
DARK OR LIGHT IS ALL IN HOW YOU USE IT. YOU TAUGHT ME THAT.
INDEED. AND SHALL I KEEP MY HEART BEATING BY MAGIC? OR REPLACE IT WITH AN ENCHANTED STONE?
REPLACE MYSELF, LITTLE BY LITTLE, WITH MAGICAL PARTS, UNTIL I'M JUST A MARIONETTE?
OR ENCHANT THIS WITHERING BODY UNTIL ALL HUMAN LIFE IS REPLACED BY MAGICAL QUICKENING. THERE'S A WORD FOR SUCH A BEING, WOODRUE.
IF I AM TO DIE, I WILL DIE WITH WHAT'S LEFT OF MY SOUL INTACT.
I NEVER THOUGHT YOU, OF ALL PEOPLE, WOULD BELIEVE IN SUCH A THING AS THE SOUL, GIVEN THE QUESTIONABLE THINGS YOU'VE DONE.
WHY NOT? I BELIEVE IN LOTS OF MAGICAL THINGS. DON'T YOU?
PERHAPS I'M A FOOL. BUT IN THE END, THE ONLY THING THAT STILL MATTERS IS TO LOOK IN A MIRROR AND SEE A MAN I DON'T ENTIRELY DESPISE.

COURTNEY TRIED TO PUT HER CONCERNS ABOUT HOLLY OUT OF HER MIND.

SHE WAS ENJOYING THE NOVELTY OF REAL COMPANIONSHIP, AND DIDN'T WANT IT SPOILED BY WHAT WAS MOST LIKELY HER OWN PARANOIA.
HEY, IT'S HOLLY, RIGHT?

WANT SOME PHRUICE?
I LOVE THAT SWEATER! DID YOU MAKE THAT?
ANGIE AND I WERE GONNA HIT THE MALL LATER. WANNA COME?
OR NOT.

WOW, THAT WAS WEIRD.
SHE DECIDED TO KEEP A CLOSE EYE ON THE NEW GIRL.

THE PROBLEM WAS THAT SHE HAD A HARD TIME SAYING NO TO HOLLY. THE PLEASURE IN SHARING WAS TOO TEMPTING.
SO YOU CAN USE THIS ONE TO MAKE SOMEONE ELSE DO YOUR HOMEWORK?
EXCEPT THE POINT OF HOMEWORK IS TO DO IT YOURSELF AND ACTUALLY LEARN SOMETHING.
THE WORST PART WAS THAT HER WORRIES WERE TAKING AWAY ALL JOY IN HER NEWFOUND FRIENDSHIP.
YOU SURE YOU DON'T WANT TO COME ALONG? AMY SAYS SHE'LL BUY US ANYTHING WE WANT.
NAH, I HAVE SOME CURDLED MILK AT HOME THAT'S EVEN MORE TEMPTING.
EACH DAY, HER FEARS GREW.
I THINK YOU'VE LEARNED ENOUGH SPELLS FOR THE TIME BEING.

IS THERE A PROBLEM?
I JUST THINK YOU NEED TO TAKE THINGS A LITTLE SLOWER.
MAGIC CAN DO STRANGE THINGS TO YOUR HEAD.
MAKE YOU THINK YOU CAN DO WHATEVER YOU WANT.
COURTNEY WAS SHOCKED AT THE HARSH WORDS COMING FROM HER OWN MOUTH.
SHE WAS USED TO CONFRONTING ENEMIES, BUT CONFRONTING SOMEONE SHE CONSIDERED A FRIEND WAS A LOT HARDER.
WHAT ARE YOU LOOKING AT?
NOTHING.
BUT WAS HOLLY A FRIEND, OR WAS SHE THE WORST ENEMY COURTNEY HAD?
UNCLE A? HOW DO YOU KNOW WHETHER YOU CAN TRUST SOMEONE?

WHAT, NOW? SORRY, I WAS MILES AWAY.
HOW DID YOU KNOW YOU COULD TRUST ME WITH WITCHCRAFT?
YOU MEAN TRUST YOU NOT TO ABUSE IT?
I DIDN'T. AND I WAS RIGHT, AS I RECALL.
WHAT IF I USED IT AGAINST YOU?
WHY WOULD YOU DO THAT?
I DON'T KNOW. BUT IF I DID...
MAYBE I'M A FOOL, BUT I THINK EVERY YOUNG WITCH SHOULD HAVE THE FREEDOM TO MAKE MISTAKES.
GOOD JUDG-MENT COMES FROM DEALING WITH THE CONSEQUENCES OF BAD JUDGMENT.
BESIDES, THERE ARE WAYS TO TAKE MAGIC AWAY IF NEED BE.
JUST BE CAREFUL I NEVER NEED TO USE THEM ON YOU.
AS EVER, UNCLE ALOYSIUS MANAGED TO BE TERRIFYING AND REASSURING AT THE SAME TIME.
BUT COURTNEY WAS RELIEVED THAT, IF WORSE CAME TO WORSE, SHE COULD HAVE HIM DEAL WITH HOLLY.

Goblin Town
NO FOOD OR DRINK BEYOND THIS POINT
MORTALS STAY OUT!
I THOUGHT I WARNED YOU TO STAY OUT OF THE FOREST.
SO THIS IS THE ENTRANCE TO GOBLIN TOWN?
WHAT WAS YOUR FIRST CLUE?
COURTNEY HAD A SINKING FEELING, AS THOUGH EVENTS WERE PULLING HER TOWARD THE INEVITABLE.
I SUPPOSE YOU WANT TO CHECK IT OUT.
I'M GAME IF YOU ARE.
SHE REALISED SHE WAS A FOOL TO HOPE ALOYSIUS WOULD TAKE CARE OF THIS. HOLLY WAS HER PROBLEM.
AND SHE HAD TO DEAL WITH IT SOONER OR LATER.

REMEMBER, WE CAN'T EAT OR DRINK ANYTHING HERE, OR WE MAY NEVER GET OUT AGAIN.
GOTCHA. THAT'S WHY I BROUGHT WATER.

THE MARKET IS THIS WAY. YOU'LL LIKE IT.
WAIT! ISN'T IT THIS WAY?

HOW'D YOU KNOW?
OH, UH, I CAN SMELL IT. CAN'T YOU?

SURE CAN.

WOW, I DIDN'T THINK THERE'D BE SO MANY OF THEM.
I'D *REALLY* HATE TO GET *TRAPPED* DOWN HERE.
IT'S NOT FUN.

GLAD WE HAVE THESE, RIGHT?
DON'T WANT TO GET TEMPTED.
YEAH. GOOD THINKING.
I'M SO SORRY, COURTNEY.
YOU OUGHT TO BE.
I SWITCHED BOTTLES.
HOPE YOU DIDN'T HAVE ANY COOTIES.

SEVENTY TO HIS DARK MAJESTY. I HAVE SEVENTY, DO I HEAR EIGHTY?
IT'S A CRYING SHAME, REALLY.
MEH?
COURTNEY! YOU'VE GOTTA LET ME OUT. PLEASE!
WHY? I SHOWED YOU NOTHING BUT FRIENDSHIP, AND YOU REPAID ME WITH LIES AND BETRAYAL.
ONLY AN IDIOT WOULD TRUST AN EVIL WITCH TWICE.
OH, I'M EVIL? ME!?!

THAT'S RICH COMING FROM YOU, COURTNEY CRUMIN!
THINK YOUR FRIEND AXEL WOULD AGREE?
WHAT DID YOU SAY?
AXEL ARTAUD. RING A BELL? HOW ABOUT ALICIA OUDLER? OR GARETH ROSSER?
WHICH OF US WOULD THEY SAY WAS THE EVIL ONE?

Chapter Three

ONCE UPON A TIME, A GIRL NAMED HOLLY HART, BORED TO TEARS WITH THE DULLNESS AND PREDICTABILITY OF LIFE, FOUND HERSELF WISHING FOR SOMETHING, ANYTHING, NEW.
IF SHE WASN'T SO TERRIFIED, SHE'D PROBABLY HAVE LAUGHED AT THE IRONY.
BUT SOMETIMES LIFE MOVES SO FAST, YOU DON'T NOTICE THE LITTLE PRANKS IT PLAYS ON YOU.
BUTTERWORM!
AND ONLY LATER DO YOU SUSPECT THAT SOME UNKIND GOD OR OTHER BEING MUST BE HAVING A LAUGH AT YOUR EXPENSE.

NEXT TIME, STICK TO THE ROAD. NO ONE WILL BOTHER YOU, I'LL SEE TO THAT.
SO MARCY WAS BEING LITERAL. YOU ARE A-
-WITCH...
HOLLY DIDN'T BOTHER TELLING HER PARENTS ABOUT THE INCIDENT. THEY BARELY LISTENED AT THE BEST OF TIMES. BESIDES, HER MEMORY OF IT WAS ALREADY GARBLED AND VAGUE.
I HEARD YOU WENT IN THE WOODS. ARE YOU OKAY?
DID YOU MEET HER? I TRIED TO WARN YOU. IT'S BEST TO JUST STAY OUT OF HER WAY.
SHE HAD NO IDEA WHAT WAS GOING ON.
AND HOLLY WAS THE SORT OF GIRL THAT NEEDED TO KNOW EVERYTHING.
OKAY, WHAT WAS ALL THAT ABOUT YESTERDAY?
YOU REALLY WANT TO KNOW?

TO HER AMAZEMENT, HOLLY FOUND HERSELF MAKING FRIENDS WITH A GIRL EVERYONE IN THE NEIGHBORHOOD SEEMED TO BE AFRAID OF.
A MAGIC STONE? YOU'RE JOKING.
JUST TAKE A LOOK.
BUT COURTNEY WASN'T REALLY FRIGHTENING AT ALL. ON THE CONTRARY, SHE WAS PROBABLY THE COOLEST GIRL HOLLY HAD EVER MET.
WOW!
PRETTY GOOD, RIGHT?
AND YOU CAN DO ALL THESE SPELLS?
BY NOW, HOLLY WAS ONLY MILDLY SURPRISED TO FIND THAT COURTNEY LIVED IN THE CREEPY OLD HOUSE NEXT DOOR.
SHE COULDN'T BELIEVE HER LUCK. AS SHE LEAFED THROUGH THE SPELLS, IT CREPT OVER HER THAT HER LIFE MIGHT NEVER BE THE SAME.
SOME OF 'EM.
WHAT ABOUT THIS ONE? LOOKS USEFUL.
Chapter Six
OH. ERRR...
AND THAT'S WHEN IT WENT WRONG.

SPELLS LIKE THIS ONE SEEM LIKE THEY MAKE LIFE *EASIER*, BUT...
HOLLY DIDN'T UNDERSTAND WHAT HAD CHANGED THE MOOD SO MUCH.
COURTNEY BECAME DISTANT, IRRITABLE, EVEN SUSPICIOUS.
WHAT COULD BE SO DANGEROUS ABOUT SO SIMPLE A SPELL? HOLLY WAS DETERMINED TO FIND OUT.
SO WHEN COURTNEY WAS IN THE BATHROOM...
Chapter Six
A FEW HOUSEHOLD HERBS AND SOME GARBLED TEXT IN AN OLD SCOTTISH DIALECT, WHICH REMINDED HER OF A SONG HER PARENTS SANG AT NEW YEAR'S.
SHE WASN'T SURE SHE WAS PRONOUNCING IT RIGHT. BUT A FOOTNOTE INDICATED THAT THE SPELL'S EFFECT WAS CREATED BY THE CASTER'S FOCUSED DESIRE.

AND JUST LIKE THAT, SHE WAS THE MOST POPULAR KID IN SCHOOL.
AT FIRST SHE FELT A LITTLE ASHAMED OF HERSELF.
ANYTHING YOU WANT. I LOVE PLAYING DRESS-UP.
YOU SHOULDN'T SPEND YOUR ALLOWANCE ON ME.
BUT AFTER REFLECTING FOR A MOMENT ON THE PHRASE "TAKING ADVANTAGE OF RICH KIDS," SHE GOT OVER IT.
ARE YOU JOKING?
ONLY ONE THING STILL CONCERNED HER.
COOL, HUH?

CATHY SAYS SHE GETS A COUPLE GRAND A MONTH JUST FOR CLOTHES. YOU SHOULD COME NEXT TIME.
NO THANKS.
I PREFER MY FRIENDSHIPS MORE HONEST.
HOLLY THOUGHT ABOUT APOLOGIZING FOR GOING BEHIND COURTNEY'S BACK.
BUT IT WASN'T LIKE SHE WAS DEPRIVING HER OF ANYTHING. WHAT WAS THE HARM?
ARE YOU CRAZY? I WARNED YOU TO STAY OUT OF HER WAY. SHE LOOKED LIKE SHE WANTED TO KILL YOU.
COURTNEY'S NOT SO BAD. JUST A LITTLE MOODY, IS ALL. IF YOU GOT TO KNOW HER...
YEAH. RIGHT.
LET ME INTRODUCE YOU TO SOMEONE WHO "GOT TO KNOW HER."

THAT'S GARETH. GO SAY HELLO.
ERR... HI THERE-
EYUGH! CRIPES!
THIS IS A FRIEND OF YOURS? WHAT'S WRONG WITH HIM?
I DON'T KNOW.
HE WAS... HE USED TO BE SO HANDSOME. YOU SHOULD HAVE SEEN HIM.
THEN HE MET COURTNEY CRUMRIN.

OF COURSE, I WASN'T EXACTLY THE NICEST PERSON-
SHUT UP, GARETH!
SEE? I EVEN HATE MYSELF WHEN I'M AROUND HIM.
SO WHY BOTHER TALKING TO HIM AT ALL?
BECAUSE NO ONE ELSE WILL.
HANG ON.
WOW...

ONE DAY IT'S A TOTALLY NORMAL BABY, THE NEXT, IT'S THE CREEPIEST KID YOU EVER SAW.
EVER SINCE SHE STARTED BABYSITTING.
AND THAT'S AXEL. HE WAS A DORK, BUT A NICE ONE.
MISSING
GUESS WHO WAS THE LAST PERSON HE WAS SEEN WITH.
HEY, MARCY.
YOU TELL HER ABOUT ALICIA?

MISS OUDLER? YOU HAVE COMPANY.
HEY, ALLIE. HOW'S IT GOING?
IT'S NOT A GOOD DAY. TRY NOT TO ALARM HER.
ALLIE? IT'S ME, SUSAN.
SHE JUST KEEPS GETTING WORSE.
WHAT'S WRONG WITH HER?
SHE HAS NIGHTMARES.
NIGHTMARES. RIGHT.

EVERY NIGHT, MONSTERS COME INTO HER ROOM AND TELL HER THAT IF SHE'S BAD, THEY'LL EAT HER.
MEDS DON'T HELP. SHE WAS IN A HOSPITAL FOR A WHILE, BUT THEY JUST FOLLOWED HER.
NIGHTMARES DID THAT?
THING IS, I STAYED OVER ONE NIGHT, TO PROVE THERE WERE NO MONSTERS. EVERY TIME I TURNED MY BACK, SHE STARTED SCREAMING.
BUT YOU DIDN'T SEE ANYTHING.
NO.
BUT I'M PRETTY SURE I HEARD THEM, SKITTERING AROUND BEHIND MY BACK.
AND YOU THINK THAT SOMEHOW, COURTNEY CRUMRIN-
AAAAAA

AAAAAAAAAAAAAAAAAAAA
DON'T SAY HER NAME!
WE USED TO BULLY OTHER KIDS FOR THEIR LUNCH MONEY.
NICE. IS THAT HOW RICH KIDS GET THEIR KICKS?
OUR FOLKS FOUND OUT WE WERE SAVING UP TO RUN AWAY, AND STOPPED OUR ALLOWANCE.
WHAT DID YOU WANT TO RUN AWAY FOR? I THOUGHT YOU GUYS ALL HAD IT MADE AROUND HERE.
THEY WOULDN'T LET US HANG OUT ANYMORE.
WHY NOT?
NONE OF YOUR BUSINESS.
ANYWAY, ALICIA TRIED IT ON COURTNEY. A FEW DAYS LATER, THIS STARTED.
WE WERE ALWAYS THE TOWN REJECTS, BUT WE HAD EACH OTHER. NOW, SHE MIGHT AS WELL BE A MILLION MILES AWAY.

IT DIDN'T MAKE SENSE. GRUMPY AS COURTNEY COULD BE, HOLLY COULDN'T RECONCILE THE GIRL SHE KNEW WITH DARK PORTRAYAL CREATED BY THE STORIES.
HAVING FUN WITH THE COOL KIDS?
OH, UM.. JUST GETTING TO KNOW THE LOCALS. THEY'RE NOT SO BAD.
RIGHT. PERFECTLY NICE RICH SNOBS THAT NEED TO BE BEWITCHED EVEN TO TALK TO YOU.
THAT WAS THE POINT HOLLY REALISED JUST HOW FRIGHTENING HER FRIEND WAS.
WHATEVER. IF THAT'S WHAT YOU WANT TO DO WITH WITCHCRAFT, I CAN'T STOP YOU.
CAN'T YOU?

WHAT WAS THAT?
NOTHING.
THAT NIGHT, HOLLY LAY AWAKE, TURNING IT ALL OVER. IT WAS PROBABLY JUST A MATTER OF TIME BEFORE SHE WOULD SUFFER THE SAME FATE AS THE OTHER KIDS. OR ONE MUCH WORSE.

SHE HAD ONLY HALF BELIEVED COURTNEY'S TALES OF HER ADVENTURES IN GOBLIN TOWN AND BEYOND.
Goblin Town

BUT THEY TURNED OUT TO BE QUITE USEFUL.
SPLAT

WHAT WAS THAT?
I KNOW NOT, SISTER, BUT IT DOTH SMELL DELICIOUS.
AS DID THE MICROWAVE LASAGNA HER MOTHER HAD LEFT HER FOR DINNER.
THE NEXT PART WAS LESS PLANNED OUT.
GOBLIN TOWN WAS A WAKING NIGHTMARE.
FRESH FRUIT, MILADY?
ERR... NO THANKS.
BUT I'M OUT OF WATER.
IN THAT CASE, CAN I INTEREST YOU IN SOME HONEYSUCKLE NECTAR?

NOW SHE KNEW WHY ALICIA HAD CRACKED UP.
Goblin Town
BEING SURROUNDED BY THOSE GOBLIN FACES JUST FOR A FEW MINUTES WAS EASILY THE MOST HARROWING EXPERIENCE OF HER LIFE.
AND IT WASN'T OVER YET.
THOUGHT I TOLD YOU TO STICK TO THE ROAD.
SHE HAD TO PLAY IT COOL. COURTNEY CRUMRIN WAS MANY THINGS, BUT SHE WASN'T STUPID.
SO... THIS IS THE ENTRANCE TO GOBLIN TOWN?
SHE SOUNDED HORRIBLY ARTIFICIAL TO HERSELF.
I SUPPOSE YOU WANT TO CHECK IT OUT.
I'M GAME IF YOU ARE.
SHE WONDERED HOW LONG IT WOULD TAKE FOR COURTNEY TO CATCH ON.
AND WHETHER BEING CAUGHT WOULD BE WORSE THAN WHAT WOULD HAPPEN IF HER PLAN SUCCEEDED.
I BROUGHT WATER.

SHE WONDERED IF SHE COULD EVER LOOK IN THE MIRROR AGAIN.
I'D REALLY HATE TO GET TRAPPED DOWN HERE.
IT'S NOT FUN.
GLAD WE HAVE THESE, RIGHT?
SHE COULD BARELY LISTEN TO THE LIES COMING FROM HER OWN MOUTH.
THAT'S WHEN SHE REALIZED THAT SHE HAD MADE A TERRIBLE MISTAKE. WHAT-EVER COURTNEY HAD DONE, OR MIGHT DO, THIS WAS NOT THE SOLUTION.
WAIT, I...

I'M SO SORRY, COURTNEY.
YOU OUGHT TO BE.
I SWITCHED BOTTLES.
AND THEN...
WHEN SHE AWOKE, IT WAS TO THE SOUND OF THE GOBLIN SLAVE AUCTION.
YOU'VE GOTTA LET ME OUT.
ONLY AN IDIOT WOULD TRUST AN EVIL WITCH TWICE.
OH, I'M EVIL? ME!?!
THINK AXEL ARTAUD WOULD AGREE?
WHAT DID YOU SAY?

SHE TRIED TO EXPLAIN WHAT SHE LEARNED ABOUT GARETH ROSSER, ALICIA OUDLER, AND AXEL ARTAUD. COURTNEY LISTENED IN SILENCE.
HOLLY DIDN'T EXACTLY EXPECT HER TO BREAK INTO TEARS OF REGRET, SO SHE WASN'T DISAPPOINTED.
AND NOW THE FULL HORROR OF HER SITUATION SUDDENLY CAME UPON HER.
SHE WANTED MORE THAN ANYTHING TO RETURN TO THE MOMENT WHEN SHE'D WISHED FOR SOMETHING NEW IN HER LIFE, AND SQUASH THE THOUGHT FOREVER.
CAN I WAKE UP NOW?
WHERE'D YOU GET THOSE?
FROM A SLEEPING GUARD.
HOW?
YOU DIDN'T THINK I'D COME DOWN HERE WITHOUT A TRICK OR-

OOF!
SMACK
REMEMBER ME, LITTLE HUMAN? NOT SO SMUG NOW, ARE YOU?
OH NO...
YOU KNOW THIS GUY?
DON'T WORRY. WE WON'T PUT YOU ON THE AUCTION BLOCK THIS TIME.

I ALREADY HAVE A BUYER LINED UP.
OH, BUGGER!
I'M SURE YOU'LL GET ALONG SPLENDIDLY.

Chapter Four

THIS IS MY WILL. IF YOU DON'T MIND, I'D LIKE YOU BOTH TO REVIEW IT NOW.
I WON'T HAVE ANY FOOLISH ARGUMENTS AFTER I'M GONE.
HOW THOUGHTFUL. I SEE YOU'RE LEAVING ME A THIRTEEN-YEAR-OLD GIRL ALONG WITH SOME NICE BOOKS AND A CAR I'LL NEVER DRIVE.
YOU NEVER APPROVED OF MY SUPERVISION OF HER. LET'S SEE IF YOU CAN DO BETTER.
WHAT ABOUT YOUR, ER, OTHER DUTIES TO THE COMMUNITY? THERE'S NO REFERENCE TO WHO WILL BE TAKING THEM OVER.
NOT EXACTLY SOMETHING ONE CAN HAND DOWN, LIKE A TASTELESS DIAMOND TIARA.
SPEAKING OF SUPERVISION, WHERE IS COURTNEY?
GOOD QUESTION.

IT IS MY TASK TO TEACH MY CHILDREN TO HUNT. NOTHING CHALLENGES A HUNTER LIKE SMART, RESOURCEFUL *PREY*.
AND WITCHES ARE THE MOST RESOURCEFUL OF *ALL* MORTALS.
I WILL GIVE YOU AN HOUR'S *HEAD START*.

DO YOU THINK THEY'LL-
ALREADY LEAVING ME BEHIND?
I DIDN'T TAKE IT PERSONALLY WHEN YOU DOSED MY WATER BOTTLE.
IF YOU WANT TO LIVE THROUGH THE DAY, YOU BETTER KEEP UP.
IT'S LIKE A LABYRINTH IN HERE.
SHOULD WE PUT MARKS ON THE TREES IN CASE WE WANT TO DOUBLE BACK?

YA KNOW, LIKE IN THE FAIRY TALES?
SURE, LET'S MAKE AN EVEN CLEARER TRAIL FOR THE WOLVES TO FOLLOW.
SO WE JUST STOP AT A GAS STATION AND ASK FOR DIRECTIONS?
ACTUALLY, THAT'S NOT A BAD IDEA. DOWN HERE, EVERYTHING IS MAGICAL.
EXCUSE ME. UH, WE'RE KINDA BEING CHASED BY WOLVES. ANY ADVICE?
YONDER RUNS THE RIVER MORPHIA. CROSS IT, AND THE WOLVES WILL LOSE YOUR SCENT.
THANKS.
UH, THAT WAS JUST A LITTLE BIT AMAZING.

I THINK I'M GOING TO HAVE TO COME UP WITH SOMETHING EVEN BETTER.
HOW ARE WE SUPPOSED TO CROSS THIS? CLIMB DOWN? THE HOUR IS ALMOST UP!
ACTUALLY, I THINK IT WAS UP A LITTLE WHILE AGO.
WHY DO YOU SAY THAT?
'CAUSE WE'RE SURROUNDED.
THAT WASN'T A VERY LONG HUNT. MAYBE THEY'LL GIVE US A DO-OVER.
DON'T BE STUP—

UH...
I REALLY HOPE YOU CAN SWIM.
WHAT-?
OKAY, MUTTS! WANT A WITCH FOR DINNER?

EAT THIS!
>GASP<
>COUGH< COURTNEY!
>COUGH< YOU JERK!

ANYONE HOME?
SORRY TO WAKE YOU, BUT I, UH, I NEED HELP.
SHE WON'T WAKE, I'M AFRAID. NOT EVER AGAIN.
WHAT?
SHE WAS ONCE A BEAUTIFUL, KINDLY MAIDEN, YOU KNOW. A THOUSAND YEARS AGO.
HER FATHER BETROTHED HER TO A CRUEL, UGLY DUKE. SO SHE CALLED TO THE TWILIGHT KING.
AND HE TOOK HER AWAY TO BE HIS DAUGHTER, AND TO BE MERRY IN HIS LAND FOREVER.

WHO ARE YOU?
I AM THE MAN WHO KILLED HER.
FOR VENGEANCE, THE TWILIGHT KING CURSED ME WITH PERFECT UNDER-STANDING OF WHAT I HAD DONE, AND WHO I HAD DONE IT TO: A SIMPLE, INNOCENT GIRL THAT LOVED ALL CREATURES AND NEVER HAD A HARSH WORD FOR ANYONE.
NO PUNISHMENT COULD BE WORSE THAN TO FALL IN LOVE WITH THE ONE WHOM YOU HAVE MURDERED.
MR. TEMPLETON?
I BROUGHT YOUR DINNER.
OH, HELLO.
WHO ARE YOU?
I'M KINDA, SORTA BEING CHASED BY WOLVES. CAN YOU GUYS HELP ME OUT?
IS THERE A FAERIE POLICE?

I MUST STAY HERE UNTIL I FIND FORGIVENESS.
OH NO!

STAY BACK!
STOP, I BEG YOU...

THIS MORTAL IS MY RIGHTFUL PREY.
JUST LEAVE US, PLEASE.

DON'T MAKE ME DO THIS.

COME AND GET IT, FIDO!

OOF!

HUH?

OH BUGGER!

RAAAAAAAAAGH!
THAT'S MY EXIT!
THIS'LL BE FUN.

HELLO!?! ANYONE HOME?
NO BIG DEAL, JUST BEING CHASED BY BLOODTHIRSTY FAERIE WOLVES! LITTLE HELP?
BEGONE, MORTAL. I'LL HAVE NO FURTHER TRUCK WITH YOUR KIND.
NOW WHAT DID I DO?
YOU TAKE EVERYTHING, AND LEAVE ONLY A TRAIL OF GRIEF.
WELL, THE SOONER YOU HELP ME, THE SOONER I'LL LEAVE YOU AND YOUR PEOPLE ALONE.
AND HOW MANY MUST SUFFER TO SAVE YOU THIS TIME?
HOW MANY HAVE YOU LEFT DYING, AS MY DAUGHTER DID, THAT YOU MIGHT ESCAPE?

HSSSSSS
GRRAAAAHH

REMEMBER ME?
ARE YOU TIRED OF RUNNING THEN, LITTLE PREY?
WITCH-FIRE, BURN.

YOUR DADDY DOESN'T GET IT. WITCHES ARE NOT YOUR PREY.
YOU ARE OURS!
CAN'T BELIEVE THEY FELL FOR THAT.
NOW, IF ONLY I THOUGHT TO LEARN SOME GOOD HEALING SPELLS.
WHOA!

HOME.
...WANNA GO HOME...
I DIDN'T KNOW WHERE ELSE TO TAKE HIM.
ANYWAY... HE BELONGS TO YOU, RIGHT?
THIS WAY.

IS HE GOING TO BE OKAY?
WHY SHOULD YOU CARE? YOU ABANDONED HIM.
HEY, I CAME BACK, DIDN'T I?
IT IS SILVER THAT POISONS HIM, FROM THE BULLET HE TOOK FOR YOU A YEAR AGO.
SOON, IT WILL CLAIM HIS FAERIE LIFE.
SORRY.
YOU'LL NEVER LEAVE ME, WILL YOU, MY LOVE.

"PLEASE, NEVER LEAVE ME."
ESSENCE OF SHE TO WHOM YOU BELONG, I SHALL FOLLOW.
DO NOT LEAD ME WRONG.
SO YOU DARE RETURN WITHOUT YOUR PREY.
SHE IS A WITCH, O FEROCIOUS FATHER. SHE IS DEADLY.
NO, THEY ARE ONLY DECEITFUL.

I AM DEADLY!
I WILL
OW YOU
HOW TO HUNT
WITCHES!

Chapter Five

ANYONE HOME?
HELLO, MISS CRUMRIN.

TEMPLETON!
STAY BACK. MY UNCLE TAUGHT ME SOME NEW TRICKS SINCE LAST TIME.
ESPECIALLY FOR JERKS LIKE YOU.
PLEASE. I WELCOME DESTRUCTION.
I THOUGHT I COULD FIND FOR- GIVENESS HERE. BUT WE'RE POISON TO THIS PLACE.
I CAN'T EVEN DO GOOD WITHOUT DOING EVIL AS WELL.
I CAN RELATE.
I'M LOOKING FOR A FRIEND OF MINE. WELL, MAYBE NOT A FRIEND. JUST ANOTHER KID I DRAGGED INTO TROUBLE.
I DIDN'T MEAN TO, BUT THAT'S HOW IT WORKED OUT.
AFTER I KILLED THE WOLF, CONSTANCE TOOK HER AWAY.

YOU DIDN'T GO WITH THEM? THEY'RE ALONE OUT THERE!
I VOWED TO STAND VIGIL HERE UNTIL I FOUND FORGIVENESS FOR MY CRIME.
AND YOU FIGURE YOU'RE GOING TO FIND IT HANGING AROUND HERE FEELING GUILTY?
YOU MUST HAVE A CONSCIENCE. HOW DO YOU LIVE WITH KNOWING WHAT EVIL YOU'VE DONE?
KNOWING YOU'LL DO MORE?
I FEEL LIKE A JERK.
BUT THEN I GET ON WITH MY LIFE, AND TRY NOT TO SCREW UP SO BAD THE NEXT TIME.
WE'RE NOT FAERIES, TEMPLETON.
WE DON'T HAVE FOREVER.

THIS IS THE WAY OUT?
A SECRET WAY, KNOWN ONLY TO THE KING AND HIS DAUGHTERS.
SHOULDN'T WE FIND COURTNEY FIRST? I CAN'T JUST LEAVE HER HERE.
I WILL FIND HER AND SEND HER HOME.
YOU'RE NOT COMING?
I CAN'T DESERT THE KING. IT'D BREAK HIS HEART.
BESIDES...
THIS IS MY HOME NOW. I DON'T BELONG UP THERE ANYMORE.
HOLLY WANTED MORE THAN ANYTHING TO ESCAPE THIS PLACE AND NEVER SEE ANYTHING MAGICAL AGAIN.

SHE WAS THE ONLY ONE WHO COULD HELP COURTNEY NOW.
BUT THE THOUGHT OF ABANDONING COURTNEY MADE HER FEEL PHYSICALLY ILL.
EXCEPT THAT WAS THE DUMBEST IDEA EVER.
SOMETIMES, BRAVERY AND NOBILITY TAKE A BACK SEAT TO COMMON SENSE.
COURTNEY HAD SAVED HER LIFE. SHE HAD TO GO BACK, HOPELESS AS THE TASK WAS.
AND THE SENSIBLE THING TO DO WAS FIND COURTNEY'S UNCLE ALOYSIUS AND EXPLAIN EVERYTHING.
IT WASN'T EXACTLY THE SOFT OPTION. SHE KNEW SHE COULDN'T WORM HER WAY OUT OF RESPONSIBILITY.
BUT WHATEVER THE OLD WARLOCK MIGHT DO TO HER...
SHE HAD TO TELL THE TRUTH AND FACE THE MUSIC.

YOU SEE? THE HUNT ISN'T *ALWAYS* A CHASE. KNOWING WHERE TO WAIT CAN BE MORE EFFECTIVE.
HEY, FIDO!

THE FIRST MUTT TO ATTACK GETS ROASTED ALIVE!
THEN WE WILL ALL ATTACK TOGETHER.
THEN YOU ALL GO UP IN ONE BIG FIREBALL.
JUST LET HER GO, AND THE FIRE GOES AWAY. YOU CAN HAVE ME.
YOU WILL SURRENDER YOURSELF?
YES.

HA! BUT WE CARE NOT FOR SURRENDER! THAT IS FOR HUMANS.
IT IS THE CHASE, THE BLOOD, THE DANCE OF LIFE AND DEATH THAT QUICKENS THE HEART OF THE HUNTER.
IF IT'S DEATH YOU WANT, I THINK I CAN OBLIGE.

YOU KNOW THAT WITCH-FIRE WILL NOT BRING TRUE DEATH TO YOUR KIND.

BUT I'M SORRY TO SAY THAT THIS WILL.

IS THAT REALLY YOUR GAME?
VERY WELL. THEY MAY GO.

AND HOW DO YOU INTEND TO ESCAPE US?
BUT WE CAN'T-
WE NEED MY UNCLE. NOW!

I DON'T. I CAME IN SEARCH OF ATONEMENT.

I'M READY.

WHAT ARE YOU WAITING FOR? GET TO MY HOUSE!
THEY WON'T CHASE US OUT HERE, WILL THEY?
YOU'RE SUCH >PUFF< AN OPTIMIST.
MUST BE NICE.
COURTNEY KNEW HER ONLY HOPE WAS TO REACH HOME IN TIME, AND SHE PRAYED THAT UNCLE ALOYSIUS COULD HELP THEM.

BUT SHE ALSO KNEW THAT HOPES WERE FOOLISH THINGS.

AND ONLY THE INDIFFERENT MOON WOULD SEE.
NO!

COURTNEY!

WELL DONE, CHILDREN. TO THE SWIFTED PAW GOES FIRST BLOOD...
YOU'RE NOT MINE!
NO, BUT THESE ARE OURS.
BACK AWAY.
WHO ARE YOU, THAT DARE STAND BETWEEN THE LORD OF THE HUNT AND HIS PREY?

PREY? MY BLOOD? MY KIN? ON MY GROUND!?!
MY NAME IS WARLOCK!!!
I AM LORD HERE, FAERIE! NOT YOU!

I KNOW I ALWAYS SAY THIS, BUT I'M REALLY GLAD TO SEE YOU, UNCLE A-
UNCLE A!?
COURTNEY, GET HELP!
GO TO RADLEY HALL. I'LL LOOK AFTER THEM.
WHO DO I GET? MR. WOODRUE?
ANYONE!

COURTNEY CRUMRIN!
OH, DEAR. MISS CRUMRIN, ARE YOU HERE?
FATHER...
TEMPLETON? GOOD GOD! WHAT HAPPENED!?!
THE TWILIGHT KING... TOLD ME I MUST FIND... ATONEMENT...
WHERE HAVE YOU BEEN? I THOUGHT YOU'D RUN AWAY...
WHO DID THIS TO YOU?
I THINK, MAYBE...
...I FOUND IT...
WHO DID THIS TO YOU?

I THOUGHT YOU WERE OKAY.
I THOUGHT YOU TOOK THAT POTION IN GERMANY.
I GAVE IT TO YOU.
WHY?
THREE BITES FROM A VAMPIRE.
IT WAS THE ONLY THING THAT WOULD SAVE YOU.
YOU SHOULD HAVE SAVED YOURSELF.
FOR ANOTHER FEW YEARS AT BEST?
I'VE HAD MY LIFETIME.
YOURS IS YET TO COME. I NEED YOU TO TAKE BETTER CARE OF IT.

ARE YOU OKAY?
FINE. HOW ARE YOU DOING?
YOU SAVED MY LIFE. I STILL DON'T GET THAT.
YEAH, THERE'S A LOT YOU'D BETTER EXPLAIN, TOO.
I'M OUTTA HERE TOMORROW. WANNA COME OVER? MEET MY AMAZINGLY CLASSY, GENIUS PARENTS?
COURTNEY, IT'S TIME TO GO HOME.
HOLLY HART?
YES?
I'M MARSHAL TRIANNE. WE HAVE SOME QUESTIONS FOR YOU.
I WANT YOU TO TELL US EXACTLY WHAT HAPPENED.

COURTNEY WOULD BE THE FIRST TO TELL YOU THAT, THOUGH ADVENTURES AND DEADLY PERIL DO WONDERS TO BUILD TRUST AMONG FRIENDS, ICE CREAM IS EASIER.
SMEDLEY HOO-HA! ICE CREAM
SMEDLEY HOO-HA
REGARDLESS, SHE WAS LOOKING FORWARD TO SEEING IF SHE REALLY HAD FOUND A REAL FRIEND IN HOLLY HART.
UH, *GOING* SOMEWHERE?
OH, *HI*. YEAH, MY DAD JUST GOT A *SIX BOOK DEAL*, AND THE *MOVIE* GOT GREEN-LIT.
SO WE'RE MOVING TO *HOLLYWOOD*.
KITCHEN
JUNK
BATHR
(UPSTAIR
KITC
IT'S *WEIRD*. ONE DAY THEY'RE SAYING THE BOOK SALES ARE *DROPPING*...
AND THEN, JUST LIKE MAGIC, *BOOM*.
YOU'RE *COURTNEY*, RIGHT?
JUN

COURTNEY CRUMRIN. YOU LIVE NEXT DOOR.
UH, YEAH, RIGHT.
SORRY WE DIDN'T GET TO KNOW EACH OTHER. YOU SEEM LIKE THE ONLY COOL KID IN THIS DUMP.
YEAH. I'M SORRY TOO.
I SUPPOSE YOU'RE HERE TO EXPLAIN WHY YOU BRAINWASHED MY FRIEND.
THEY KNOW, COURTNEY.
THE COUNCIL KNOWS EVERYTHING.
YOU'VE GOT TO GET AS FAR FROM HILLSBOROUGH AS POSSIBLE.
WHY?

YOU NEED TO ASK? YOU SUMMONED RAWHEAD AND BLOODY BONES TO MURDER A COVEN MARSHAL!
YEAH, BUT HE WAS A HUGE JERK!
COURTNEY!!!
THESE PEOPLE AREN'T ON YOUR SIDE. WITHOUT ALOYSIUS TO PROTECT YOU...
COURTNEY WAS HARDLY SURPRISED. ALL HER LIFE, SHE'D FELT HELPLESS IN A COLD WORLD WITH NO ONE TO PROTECT HER.
YEAH, I GET IT.
FOR JUST A LITTLE WHILE, SHE THOUGHT THAT HAD CHANGED, AND SOMEONE WOULD LOOK OUT FOR HER UNTIL SHE BECAME STRONG ENOUGH TO LOOK OUT FOR HERSELF.
SHE FELT A FOOL FOR EVEN THINKING IT.
STUPID, STUPID!
WHERE ARE YOU GOING?

YOU DON'T THINK I WAS SENDING YOU OFF ALONE, DO YOU?
COME ON. MY CAR IS THIS WAY.
WHY ARE YOU DOING THIS?
I PROMISED ALOYSIUS I'D KEEP YOU OUT OF TROUBLE.
WELLCOME TO HILLSBOROUGH
THAT WASN'T A SMART MOVE. HEY, YOU SAID YOU DROVE A BORING OLD VOLVO OR SOMETHING.
THIS IS A VOLVO. BUCKLE UP TIGHT AND HANG ON.

I KNOW THE WHOLE STORY, ALOYSIUS.
THE CHILDREN SHE CURSED. THAT CHANGELING IN EERIE LANE.
TEMPLETON.
TELL ME, OLD FRIEND...
WHAT DOES ONE DO WITH A SORCERER WHO BREAKS COVEN LAW?
MIGHT I REMIND YOU THAT SHE'S JUST A THIRTEEN-YEAR-OLD GIRL.
WHO CURSES OTHER CHILDREN, OR LEADS THEM INTO THE GOBLIN UNDERWORLD, SOME NEVER TO BE SEEN AGAIN.
WHO SUMMONED A HOBGOBLIN TO MURDER A COVEN MARSHAL!
IT'S ALL IN TEMPLETON'S NOTES. WHAT I WONDER IS...
HOW MUCH DID YOU ALREADY KNOW ABOUT?

AND HOW MUCH DID YOU PUT HER UP TO?
DON'T BE RIDICULOUS. THIS IS ALL HEARSAY.
SORCERERS HAVE BEEN SENTENCED TO DEATH FOR LESS. BUT YOU KNOW ALL ABOUT THAT, DON'T YOU?
YOU'RE IN LUCK, OLD FRIEND. THE COVEN REQUIRES YOUR SERVICES.
BRING THIS WAYWARD WITCH TO HEEL AND SEE THAT SHE IS PREVENTED FROM DOING FURTHER HARM, AND WE WILL CONTINUE TO PROVIDE ELIXIR VITAE.
AFTER FIFTY YEARS OF FRIENDSHIP, THIS IS HOW YOU TREAT ME?
IT IS FOR FRIENDSHIP'S SAKE THAT I SEND YOU ON THIS ERRAND AT ALL. FAIL, AND WE SHALL DISPATCH A NEW ENFORCER...
...WHO WILL DOLE OUT A PUNISHMENT FIT FOR SORCERERS THAT DEFY RAVANNA'S LAW.

Courtney Crumrin

By Ted Naifeh

The Witch Next Door

Bonus Material & Cover Gallery

Cover artwork for *Courtney Crumrin* issue #1.

Cover artwork for *Courtney Crumrin* issue #2.

Cover artwork for *Courtney Crumrin* issue #3.

Cover artwork for *Courtney Crumrin* issue #4.

Cover artwork for *Courtney Crumrin* issue #5.

A design for a potential Courtney Crumrin t-shirt.

for
Marisa